To my grandchildren,
Ada, Lucien, and Isabel
AL

To children of all ages with inquiring minds
OP

To Mink and Farve and Nanny
SC

ADA AND THE GALAXIES

ALAN LIGHTMAN *and* **OLGA PASTUCHIV**

illustrated by
SUSANNA CHAPMAN

mit Kids Press

Ada loves the stars.

But in New York, the city lights
make the night sky too bright
to see the stars.

After the long winter months, Ada and her mom
go to visit her grandparents, Ama and Poobah.

They live on an island in Maine, where the night sky is very dark and Ada can see lots of stars.

"Can we see the stars tonight?" says Ada. "I've been waiting all winter."

"Of course," says Poobah. "We'll do that as soon as it gets dark. There are lots of other things we can do in the daytime. Let's go down to the shore."

"That's the biggest nest I've ever seen," says Ada.

"Ospreys live in that nest," says Ama. "They catch fish to feed their babies. And you can hear that they don't like us to get too close."

"Let's go kayaking. I love kayaking," says Poobah.

"Me too," says Ada. "But when will we be able to look at the stars?"

"See that big rock over there?" says Poobah. "That's how I tell time on the island. Today, when it's completely covered with water, it'll be dark enough to see the stars."

"Look at these shells and bits of moss," says Ama.

"They're beautiful," says Ada. "There's a crab. Hi, little guy."

Ada goes to look at Poobah's rock. It's partly covered with water. "It's not time yet to look at the stars," says Ada.

"Let's make a fairy house with all these shells and moss we've collected," says Ama.

"Good idea," says Ada. "Maybe Crabbie can live in our fairy house."

Ada goes to look at Poobah's rock again. "It's *still* not time to look at the stars," she says. "I've been waiting and waiting."

"No, not yet," says Ama. "But it's almost dinnertime."

"It's finally, *finally* dark," says Ada.

"But where are the stars?
I've waited a *very* long time."

"I'm really sorry, " says Ama. "It seems that fog has rolled in. The weather people said the fog will be here until tomorrow."

"Maybe they're wrong," says Ada.

"Sometimes they are," says Poobah, laughing. "I have an idea. Let's look at pictures of stars."

"I don't want to look at pictures," says Ada.

"These are galaxies," says Poobah.

"What's a galaxy?" asks Ada.

"A galaxy is a lot of stars swarming around one another like bees," says Poobah. "About one hundred billion stars."

"Galaxies are far, far away, in outer space," says Poobah.

"What are these swirly things?" asks Ada. "I want to spin around and around on that swirly thing."

"If you did, you'd be going about a million miles per hour," says Poobah.

"No problem," says Ada. "Watch how fast I can spin."

"Here's another galaxy," says Poobah.

"It looks like a crab," says Ada.

"It's a very big crab," says Poobah. "About ten million million billion times bigger than the crabs you saw."

"I want to go there," says Ada. "Can we go there in a rocket ship?"

"It's pretty far," says Poobah. "It would take about a million million years to get there."

"Let's start tomorrow morning," says Ada.

"We'll have to pack a lot of snacks," says Poobah.

"Do galaxies have seashells and moss?" asks Ada.

"They probably do," says Poobah.

"Why?" asks Ada.

"Because everything in the universe is made out of the same stuff," says Poobah. "It's all part of nature. Even things that we can't see."

"Do galaxies have people?" asks Ada.

"Not people like you and me," says Poobah. "But *some* kind of people."

"I think they're lonely so far away," says Ada.

"They might be looking at us right now wondering if *we're* lonely,"
says Poobah.

"We're not lonely, are we, Poobah?"

"No, we're not."

"It's really late," says Ama. "Come and get your pj's on."

"I want to see the fairy house before I go to sleep," says Ada.

"Ama and Poobah," shouts Ada.
"The fog's gone. I can see the stars!
Wow! Come look. Come look."

"Hello, you other people," says Ada.

"Hello," says Poobah.

"Good night, you other people," says Ada.

SEEING THE NIGHT SKY

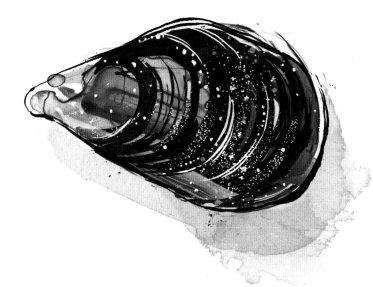

The photographs of galaxies that Poobah and Ada look at were taken with a big telescope called the Hubble Space Telescope, named after the American astronomer Edwin Hubble. In 1990, the Hubble telescope was launched into space in a rocket ship, and it has been orbiting the earth ever since. It takes clearer photographs than telescopes on the ground because it is above the earth's air, which jitters and causes slightly blurry pictures. The pictures taken by the Hubble telescope are digitized and sent by radio back to earth. The first telescope to look at the sky was made by the Italian scientist Galileo about four hundred years ago.

An average galaxy has about one hundred billion stars, all moving at high speed and attracting one another by gravity. Our sun is in a galaxy called the Milky Way. If you go outside on a clear and dark night, you can see a faint milky band of light that crosses the sky—that's the Milky Way. Every star in the sky is a sun, like our sun. Eventually, every star will use up its energy and grow dark and cold, but that won't happen to our sun for another 5,000,000,000 to 8,000,000,000 years. Astronomers think that most stars in outer space have planets orbiting around them, just as in our solar system. Some of those planets probably have living plants and animals, but life has not yet been discovered beyond Earth. Many scientists are now searching for life on other planets.

The numbers Poobah uses to describe the size and distance of galaxies are scientifically accurate.

CREDITS FOR PHOTOS USED WITHIN ILLUSTRATIONS

"These are galaxies," says Poobah: NGC 2841: NASA, ESA, and the Hubble Heritage Team (STScI/AURA)

"What are these swirly things?" asks Ada; "No problem," says Ada; front cover:
IC 342: T. A. Rector/University of Alaska Anchorage, H. Schweiker/WIYN, and NOAO/AURA/NSF

"Here's another galaxy," says Poobah; "Not people like you and me," says Poobah; front and back covers:
NGC 1300: NASA and the Hubble Heritage Team (STScI/AURA)

. . .

Text copyright © 2021 by Alan Lightman and Olga Pastuchiv
Illustrations copyright © 2021 by Susanna Chapman

The MIT Press, the ☰ mit Kids Press colophon, and MIT Kids Press are trademarks of Massachusetts Institute of Technology and used under license from The MIT Press. The colophon and MIT Kids Press are registered in the US Patent and Trademark Office.

First edition 2021

Library of Congress Catalog Card Number pending
ISBN 978-1-5362-1561-8

21 22 23 24 25 26 CCP 10 9 8 7 6 5 4 3 2 1

Printed in Shenzhen, Guangdong, China

This book was typeset in Arno.
The illustrations were created with watercolor, photos by the Hubble Space Telescope, and a digital assist.

MIT Kids Press
an imprint of Candlewick Press
99 Dover Street
Somerville, Massachusetts 02144

www.candlewick.com
www.mitkidspress.com